HELLO
OCEAN

Pam Muñoz Ryan ❧ Illustrated by Mark Astrella

W9-CAN-228

TALEWINDS

A Charlesbridge Imprint

Hello, ocean,
my old best friend.

I'm here,
with the five of me, again!

I **see** the ocean,
gray, green, blue,
a chameleon
always changing hue.

Amber seaweed,
speckled sand,

bubbly waves
that kiss the land,

wide open water
before my eyes,

reflected in a
bowl of skies,

glistening tide pools
and secret nooks—
I love the way
the ocean **looks**.

I **hear** the ocean,
a lion's roar,
crashing rumors
toward the shore,

water
shushing
and
rushing
in,

then
whispering
back to
the sea
again.

Froggy songs from distant boats,
gentle clangs from bobbing floats,

screak of gulls
calling down—

I love the way
the ocean **sounds**.

I **touch** the ocean,
and the surf gives chase,
then wraps me in a wet embrace.

Pulling,
pushing,
the restless sea
repeats the same
refrain to me.

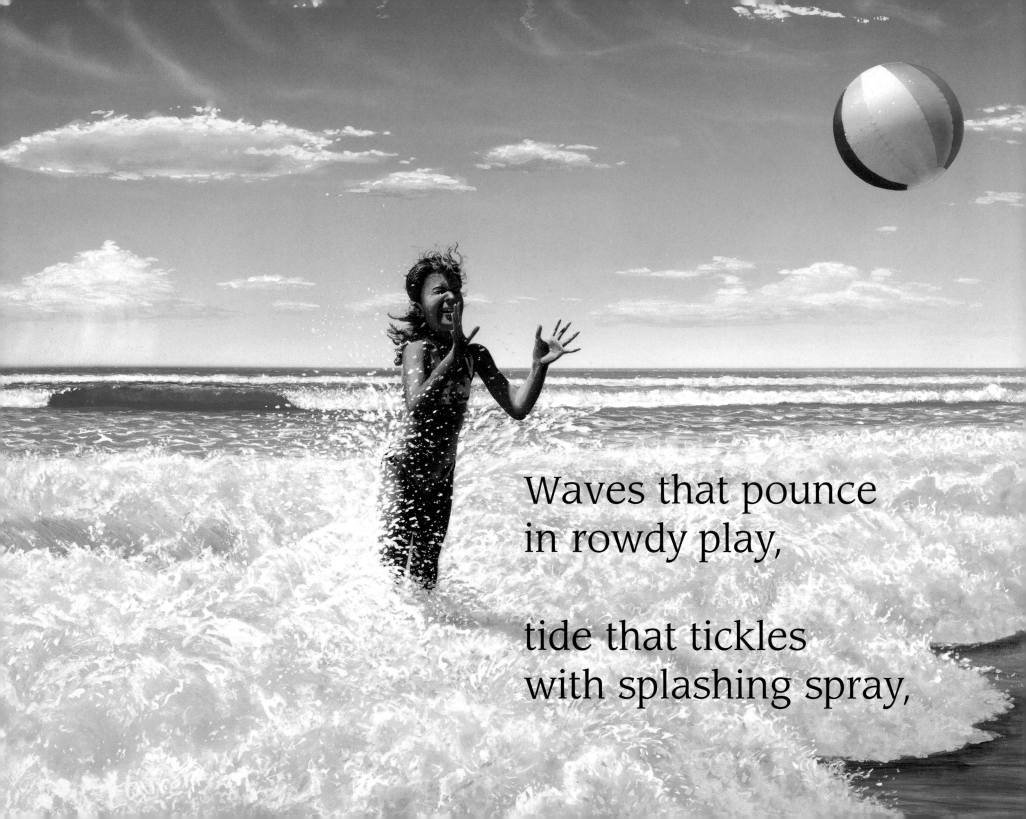

Waves that pounce
in rowdy play,

tide that tickles
with splashing spray,

squishy,
sandy,
soggy ground,

slippery seaweed that wraps around,

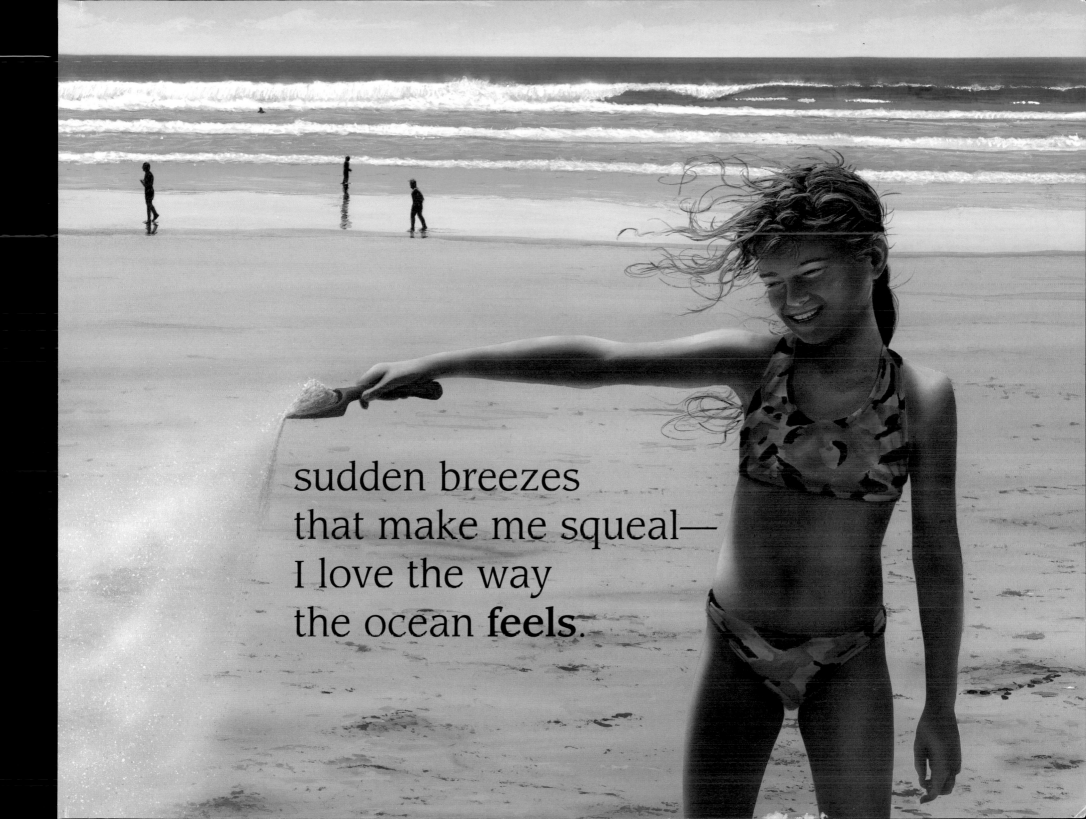

sudden breezes
that make me squeal—
I love the way
the ocean **feels**.

I **smell** the ocean,
the fresh salt wind,
wafting lotions
from suntanned skin.

Aromas from some ancient tale
disclose their news when I inhale.

Reeky fish from waters deep,

fragrant ore from holes dug steep,

drying kelp
and musty shells—
I love the way
the ocean **smells**.

I **taste** the ocean
and wonder why
it tastes like tears
I sometimes cry.

Sandy grains in a salty drink

are best for fish and whales, I think.

I lick the drops
still on my face;
I love the way
the ocean **tastes**.

The sun dips down;
it's time to go.
But I'll be back
to see your show,

hear the stories you have to spin,
taste your flavors once again,

take deep sniffs
of briny air,
and feel the treasures
you have to share.

Goodbye, ocean,
my old best friend. . . .

To Nikki and Natalie Connor, gracious and patient models,
and to the birthday girls: Sally, Kim, Barbara, and Evelyn.
—P.M.R.

For Alex and Joey, Allyssa and Ryan, Sean and Devon, Lauren,
Phoebe, and Jacob, Angel Mae and Maria Lanakila, Susan D. and
every kid who picks up a crayon or paintbrush and makes a picture!
—M.A.

Text copyright © 2001 by Pam Muñoz Ryan
Illustrations copyright © 2001 by Mark Astrella
All rights reserved, including the right of reproduction
in whole or in part in any form.

A TALEWINDS Book
Published by Charlesbridge Publishing
85 Main Street, Watertown, MA 02472
(617) 926-0329
www.charlesbridge.com

Library of Congress Cataloging-in-Publication Data
Ryan, Pam Muñoz
    Hello Ocean/Pam Muñoz Ryan; illustrated by
Mark Astrella.
        p.   cm.
    "A Talewinds book."
Summary: Using rhyming text, a child describes the wonder
of the ocean experience through each of her five senses.
    ISBN 0-88106-987-6 (reinforced for library use)
    ISBN 0-88106-988-4 (softcover)
[1. Ocean—Fiction. 2. Sense and sensations—Fiction.
3. Stories in rhyme.] I. Astrella, Mark, ill. II. Title.
PZ8.3.R955He   2001
[E]—dc21   98-15983

Printed in South Korea
(hc) 10 9 8 7 6 5 4 3
(sc) 10 9 8 7 6 5 4

Illustrations done in acrylics on airbrush paper
Display type and text type set in Goudy Oldstyle and Leawood
Color separations made by Sung In Printing, South Korea
Printed and bound by Sung In Printing, South Korea
Production supervision by Brian G. Walker
Designed by Paige Davis